EXERCISES
IN CONTROL

EXERCISES IN CONTROL
ANNABEL BANKS

Influx Press
London

Published by Influx Press
The Greenhouse
49 Green Lanes, London, N16 9BU
www.influxpress.com / @InfluxPress

First edition 2020. Printed and bound in the UK by TJ International.

Paperback ISBN: 9781910312476
Ebook ISBN: 9781910312483

Editor: Gary Budden
Assistant Editor: Sanya Semakula
Proofreader: Trudi Suzanne Shaw
Cover design: Luke Bird
Interior design: Vince Haig

*To my beautiful mama, who gave me
everything except green eyes.*

CONTENTS

PAYMENT TO THE UNIVERSE

Margaret is the boss, so you suppose it's okay that she leaves early. Actually, you're glad. By five to six the offices are empty, quiet aired. The cupboard of cleaning supplies is just large enough for a chair to fit between the boxes of bleach and stinky rags, so you can sit and look at the list of jobs for that night. Margaret is always careful to mark up the set of instructions on the dry-wipe board. They are always the same, so you don't know why she bothers. Sometimes it's written in red, sometimes in blue, but closes with the same smiley-face whose smile is more pointed than a curve. It means business.

You drop your tabard over your head, screw in your earbuds – *blue, blue, electric blue* – and drag the vacuum cleaner from its corner. Atrium first, then the halls, sucking the day's skin cells from the nylon pile. The first room is meant for visitors. Photographs of rural landscapes, oil wells, some school prize-giving where everyone is in animal masks, have been blown-up, poster size, and bolted to the wall. You rub a cloth over the fields and faces. Turn out the light when you leave.

The second is more of a kitchen, although there are no appliances. Thai food in plastic boxes, piles of fruit, apples and bananas arranged in balanced displays. On the far wall, rows of toothbrush holders have been fixed to cheap plastic shelving. You counted them once, when you were either curious or bored. Thirty across, five rows down. One hundred and fifty brushes, and never enough toothpaste. In the evening's hush you can take a moment here. You bring out your own brush from the pocket of your tabard and have a cheeky scrub, give some minty spit to the bin you then tie up and lug downstairs to the skip.

Up some stairs, down some stairs. *Blue, blue,* in your ears, and you're not allowed inside this room at all, but that's why you come here. An accident of opportunity gave you pass, and you're not about to give it up with any fake attempt at decency, of notions of 'the right thing' so carefully primed in your childhood. There is a water jug on the safe with three glasses, but you know better than to touch it. A pile of papers to shuffle, straighten, glance through. A fleshy lump in the corner, quivering, a bag on its head.

It's this last you've come to stare at. You cough loudly, so it knows that you are here, so it will call out in that language you don't understand. Doesn't matter what the words mean. You know it wants to be touched, to be able to see. The twitching is less than yesterday, even less than the day before, but perhaps that's acceptance rather than anything more final.

You think about touching it, as always. Consider uncovering its eyes, letting it take an unrestricted breath, to moisten its lips with water. Daydreaming these actions always makes you feel kinder. It's a payment to the universe, so perhaps the cigarette you'll have on your walk home won't be the one to give you cancer. Perhaps the earlier bus has been delayed just enough that you can catch it and avoid waiting in the dark, singing *pale blinds drawn all day*.

You close the door and make it back to the cupboard. Your mouth is still too minty for smoking, so you'll grab a coffee from the machine by the second floor toilets. The price has gone up, but you're not about to complain. You like this job. It fits with the hours you keep.

SUSAN
FRANKIE
MARLA
ME

The next morning my guy is early into work, but I have to get home anyway, because I'm shopping with Susan. Big Asda, not the high street. We like it in here because the wide aisles can contain our conversations, and the ceiling is high enough to cope if she gets the giggles.

We put the baskets over our arms, rest the handles in the crooks of our elbows. This is not the best way to carry them but she makes it so sexy I have to copy her, to fake being gracefully awkward with the thoughtless space-taking and the – surely not deliberate – clack and connect with baskets of men who take her fancy, fancy her back. How can they not? She's so cool in her small clothes, her loose-hipped flip-flop shuffle, peering at pomegranates, giving figs a friendly squeeze.

I'm a proper Susan-copier today. Just tactile and spacey enough to stroke a kiwi fruit, even though I feel like a tit. But I always get like this, my debilitating, just-fucked character drowsiness. Invasion, Germaine calls it. Probably, but an invited one, to distract from all the blood and drudgery. The way I see it, I'll still have to negotiate terms, clear up the tank-crushed flowers. Might as well enjoy the parade first.

Have you tried these? Susan asks, picking up white bread rolls, all-butter shortbread biscuits, white-chocolate mice. They're fabulous.

Why is it that pale things are always the worst for you?

You want Cad-burries? She runs her hand over the swell of my hip. You're feeling different, huh? Set your sheet music on fire?

There might have been some smouldering. Too early to tell if it'll catch.

Keep blowing and see what happens, she says. That's the funnest way to find out.

We open a jar of gherkins and share them, with vinegar-fingered, loud-crunch laughter, then look for lube on the vitamin shelves. Take two bottles, one each.

The freezer section is cold, and our nipples stand proud beneath our thin cotton tops. She shifts her basket to the other arm, sticks a finger out and presses, hard, on my right tit. Ding-dong, she says, American voice resonating through this British version of a Walmart palace. Are you home? Boob inspector.

A bald man, trolley laden with paper towels, had caught the action out of the corner of his eye, and pauses, mid-step, to watch. The freezers are throwing out a low hum. I think it's them, anyway, and then I'm pressing my lips to hers. She smiles into my kiss, knows what I am asking. We turn to stare him out – an invitation, a warning. I run my tongue over my lips to taste her tacky gloss, then choose Caramel Choo-Choo Ben and Jerry's. We can open the carton as we drive home. We can lick each other's fingers clean.

Come on, she says as we load the conveyor. What's he really like?

Tricksy, in a good way, I say. Pretty playful. Big male body, slightly odd-eyed. Mad grin. Has a thing about religion.

Are we doing the same guy? Her hair is almost pink, moves over her shoulders, gets in her mouth.

We're not. We check, comparing verified statistics, descriptions of cock-curve and coffee preference. I'm glad. If forced to choose between me and Susan, cello burner, ceiling toucher, I would choose her. She wears the basket in the crook of her arm. She eats gherkins she hasn't paid for and doesn't give a fuck.

▼

Frankie picks me up in her convertible. It's a huge machine, leathered, finned and roaring, not the type of car ever seen on British roads. She is stunning, as always. Her dark glasses, floral headscarf, are some sort of fifties thing I don't get, but it's the Jackie-O dresses I really enjoy. I wore them all the time when I was younger.

Are we going to make it? I ask.

Honey, she replies. I'm never late. Relax.

The car is so large I slip around in my seat, despite the belt. Don my scarf, my leopard-print shades. I have to, because the LA sunshine has followed her here.

She pulls up at the traffic lights, reaches into her bag, pulls out a leg-shaver and buzzes it over her calves. She is driving in bare feet, red toenails on the pedals. It's the most feminine thing I have ever seen. We flip the mirrors, apply lipstick. The cars behind us toot – the lights have been green for a while now – but she is unflustered, blots with a tissue before driving on. I decide not to worry about the time. I am a Frankie-copier today, and it feels good.

So, what's he like? She is picking at her eyelashes, the best that she can do under these circumstances – still better than hours of effort from me.

A bit fake, I say, but gentle enough. On a mission. Loses his head when stressed. I think back over the last two weeks. Oh, he takes instruction when it suits him but wanders away a lot. Think he's built for loneliness.

Are we doing the same guy? she asks and pulls her scarf back to sit around her throat. Her hair is dark, fake red. It is sculpted into eighties glam. It doesn't move, and I love that stiffness, because it is the only thing about her that is constrained.

We're not. We check. The same statistics, the habits that won't be faked. Come-faces and breakfast choice. The placing of hands when we're kissed.

We pull into the car park and she presses a button, gets the hood to whirr over our heads, connect with a clunk. I unbuckle my belt, grab her legs and pull them over my lap. We have time for this.

So is he your Mister Right? she asks. My fingers can't stop moving over her smooth calf, her tender knee, the softness at the back of her thigh. I'll be putting my tongue there in a minute, if I can wriggle her out of her Jackie-O dress.

I don't know how to answer that question. I look for analogies, for previous inputs, but there's nothing with enough positive valence to activate my mouth.

▼

Marla and I are sneaking into the only group that's running at this hour. We have been down the pub for a swift one, of course, so gargle mouthwash, chew the bubble-gum flavoured sugar-free gum I keep in my bag.

This shit is such a lie, she says, meaning the gum. I lurve it, baby. To me, her accent sounds false, but what do I know? I only spend time with pretend Americans.

There are about thirty people in the room. All of them turn to watch us come in, and smile, and nod. Marla is prettier than me. She gets all the winks.

I like to let them try to thirteen-step me, she whispers, spreading the word by spreading my legs. Love thy neighbour, fuck her ass.

Isn't it 'covet'?

You only covet things you're not allowed to fuck. But shh.

We listen to the prayers, to the shares. We nod along, agree to keep it simple, fill up on coffee and handshakes.

Later, when we are in her filthy bed, orange-juice stains and sticky-rib boxes, she rolls over onto her knees and tells me to pray with her. I don't recognise the words. She might be making them up, I think, but their fluidity suggests otherwise, especially the part about this numbersnake who counts the universe. Or something. I stumble, make mistakes. She says amen.

Those people kill me, she says, climbing back over my hips. Do you know what my higher power is?

Haven't a clue.

Lying. I surrender myself to the making up of shit, based on shit that I've done, or want to do. It's the only way to work out what you want.

I'm not sure if I believe her, but I suppose that's the point. She is very good at lying, but has lines that she won't cut.

Is it a lie that her hair is dark, that it leaves greasy stains on our pillow? That she wants me? Her touch moves between false-clutching anger and the pilgrim-snail's progress, a journey of redemption between spit-wet legs.

She talks about the man she is dating. Or not. She's not sure. Called her a cunt. Sent her a text to say he's sick of looking at her. Doesn't sound all there.

Are we seeing the same guy? I ask, only half-playful, but we never get the chance to find out, because it's time to dress, argue our way into that dark room, and get them to hit us, as hard as they can, for as long as we can take it. But I'm not supposed to talk about that.

EXERCISES IN CONTROL

The microwave reboils last night's cup of tea as he takes the coin from the special place and balances it, rim up, on the kitchen table. This is important. When he's at the station, deep underground and unable to absorb the vibrations with his flesh, the coin becomes him: a sacrifice to keep the city's passing planes from shattering plates, cracking the plaster, or disturbing the spider plant's raiding tendrils that have curled round the radiator, spilled across the floor.

He is afraid to prune the plant. He doesn't believe in moving flats. So he does this, and on each return opens his brown notebook, the one with the sailing ship on the front, and records how the coin landed.

Heads or tails.

▼

The green-coated girl always stands with her toes over the warning line. He wants to tell her to keep back, but the microphone would be too loud on the empty platform. Officious. Overkill. Mark him as weak. Yet he can't approach, either. He fantasises about tapping her shoulder, just where the frizzy hair covers her bag strap. She's quite small. He could lean down and smile into her face. *It's for your own safety.*

No, it's better to watch, as long as no one catches him in this inability to do his job.

She rocks back and forth on her low heels, pulling bread, or dough, or cake from a paper bag and chewing as she moves. He knows her lips are just inside-out skin, but they are pale and smooth. He thinks about her day ahead; the other factory workers, the old men on the ward. He imagines them looking at her lips. And then she takes another bite and throws the last pinch down onto the rails.

Indigestion leaps into his throat. His tongue burns with sick. Should tell her off for littering, collect evidence and call the community police people to write her up, immediate sixty-pound fine, all calm voices and stab vests. He has a walkie-talkie. They could be here in minutes, writing the ticket in front of him, and she would sigh, raise her eyes to whatever god the tunnel roof allowed and bemoan her minimum wage, the low meals now forced even lower, twelve-pence packets of chicken noodles, thrice-strained teabags, pappy white bread.

The train comes. She gets on it and is gone.

▼

The next morning, he is ready. She will drop the food, he will chastise her, and at the same time tell her to stand back from the edge. She arrives, green coat, fizzing hair, and soon begins tossing her crumbs down onto the rails. He is just stepping forward, throat already clicking, when his eye catches movement, tracks the flick of a tail, the furtive scurry, the brown fur. He watches the mouse. Watches the girl feeding the mouse.

▼

His shift ends at one, and he is home by twenty past. The coin has landed on its face. He puts the fish pie in the microwave and stares down into the queen's eye, thinking about the girl, her lips, her toes, then takes the notebook from his pocket. The column is full. The pie will still be a few minutes, journeying on its invisible waves, so he takes a seat at the table and draws a line down the centre of a new page. He means to insert a tick in the 'head' column, but instead draws a small, ink-furred body, with a tail so farcically long it spreads back over the previous pages.

▼

Monday morning brings the girl with the green coat, and he almost smiles, but stops himself just in time. Things are not going well. He'd gone for a walk by the canal yesterday, but when he got back, he saw that the coin had refused to decide, was still refusing, even. All night it stood on its rim, despite the planes that seemed to crash into his kitchen. This morning he'd touched the table with his thigh, almost an accident, but only managed to scald his chest with microwaved tea. He wants to show her the mark, but she seems to be crying. Takes a step towards her. Takes a step back. Watches her wipe her eyes with her wrist while taking another bite of bread.

Oh yes. The bread is present. A finger's worth is tossed down to the mouse he knows must be there, perhaps begging on its back legs, paws together, pleading, thanking, the tail leaving serpent-marks in the grime. The girl weeps, and feeds, and rocks forwards, and just before the train comes her heels are an inch from the marker of safety.

She pitches forward. He sees the driver shout, mouth round as a tunnel, but then she steps back just in time, hair puffed over her face by the sooty wind.

▼

That afternoon, having waved goodbye to his replacement, he sets off into town. The pet shop is in a retail complex two bus rides away, and he resents seeing his travelcard credit tick down, but it's better than walking.

The girl who serves him is small with wide brown eyes. She shows him the glass tanks at the back, the sleepy pink noses popping out from miniature castles, white fur stuck with sawdust and tiny pellets of shit.

'Don't you have any brown ones?'

'Sorry, only white. They're the most popular.' The girl's tongue is pierced, and she sticks the bar out at him, thinking. 'I've seen some. We can order one for you, but it might take a few weeks.' As she speaks, she catches one of the creatures and hands it to him. With a head the size of his thumbnail, it curls in his palm, curves the fine tail across his wrist. He runs a finger the wrong way over its fur, the skin underneath blood-filled, marvelling at this tiny sack of organs, its raspberry heart.

It's so cheap: a few pounds for a living thing. He thinks of the coin, and he knows, back at the flat, it's still standing, despite the petrol explosions, the electric shocks and jet engine roars. 'I'll take this one.'

'Would you like to see the cages?' The girl smiles down at the mouse in his hands, her fingertip rubbing at the spot between its ears.

He is glad not to look her in the eye. 'I have one at home. My little boy's mouse died, and this is its replacement. I was hoping for brown, so he wouldn't find out, but…'

She pops the mouse into a carton, folds the lid and hands it to him. 'So sad. But animals are a good way for children to learn about death, aren't they?'

He pays, thanks her, and leaves to catch the first of his buses.

▼

After slamming the front door as hard as he can, he stomps into the kitchen, heavy boots pounding on the stained linoleum. The coin remains proud. He thinks about picking it up, to check the edge of the table for sticky substances, for a drop of ketchup or mashed potato that had dried into mortar, but he decides against it. Whatever happens, he mustn't interfere.

The coffee is strong, made with two heaped tablespoons of granules, but he doesn't add milk because this is not for him to drink. After it has sat by the kettle for an hour he dips his elbow past the lip of the mug to test the liquid's temperature, opens the carton, takes the mouse by its tail and dunks it as you would a biscuit, slapping his palm over the top of the cup. The creature claws him as he tries to get its head to go under, so he lifts it by the tail, holds it over the sink, and pours the rest over in baptism, until the sawdust-sweet fur becomes a false, bitter brown.

Once back in the carton the mouse seems fine, except for a few sneezes, so he takes his other purchase, a solid pair of kitchen scissors, and sets up on the counter. It's frustrating not to be able to use the kitchen table but the coin must not be disturbed. He places cling film over the surface, sticking its edges to the lap underneath, then looks around the flat for something to make walls with, wishing he ate cereal or read books. Eventually, he trudges downstairs to the recycling bank to find some flattened cardboard, climbing the stairs back up to his flat, out of breath and wheezing.

The box is reshaped, the bottom flaps cut away. He lets the mouse run around inside this homemade cage, and each time it climbs the sides – surprisingly quick, even though it hasn't had any food or water for six hours – he knocks it down with the handle of the scissors. After watching for a while, he drops a crust of bread and strokes the top of the soft head as it eats. The little thing is quite tame; it must have been handled regularly. The girl had done a good job. He imagines her standing by the tanks, tongue piercing clattering against her teeth, dozens of mice streaming through her fingers, and it's like watching her swim through milk. It was nice to think that, if he'd had had a son, she wouldn't have sold him something dangerous.

He brings the scissors up over the mouse's back and cuts the creature in half, across its middle. The legs kick for a few seconds. He lets the blood collect in the plastic. There isn't much at all.

▼

The next morning, he gets into work early and lowers himself down onto the rails. He tries to guess where the girl in the green coat will stand, a few feet down from the entrance, opposite a poster where happy couples, smiling children and cartoon animals rotate their sentry duty every few weeks. He lays the two halves of the mouse out, centring the split so that she will see it side on when she looks down.

He stands back, appraising his work. What has he missed? It looks too clean, too surgical. The scissors were sharp. He gets his fingers up inside the front half of the mouse and pulls at some of the chilled entrails, spreading them out. Finally, because the blood had congealed in the fridge overnight, he pulls the can of coke from his pocket and spills a corona of liquid around the corpse. He climbs back onto the platform.

The girl in the green coat is on time. She stands a few feet away from where he has arranged the mouse, and he's trying to think of a way to move her down – should he approach? Point out the body? – when he sees her pull the packet of bread from her coat pocket and begin her walk, looking down into the deep well of metal and grime.

He knows the exact moment she sees the body. She stiffens. Her hair sparks more than usual, seeming to spit fire from its ends. An empty hand reaches to her mouth, not to feed but to cover.

The train is approaching. The girl is still proud, but tottering. Her green coat hitches, briefly, at the shoulder.

He takes out his notebook.

RITE
OF
PASSAGE

I suppose it was a date. A second date, so I picked her up. Not from her house, though. From outside the pub on the high street. 'Smells nice in here,' she said as she climbed in, her hair wind-blown and chaotic.

I accepted her kiss on the cheek, which made me feel giddy and grown-up at the same time. 'Does it?'

I knew it did, because I'd been all morning at the car wash. I'm not saying it was some filthy mess: I'm just saying I made an effort. She was that sort of possibility. Our first meeting had been fun, coffee, a few laughs, some anecdotes and work chat – all very easy. But I knew how fragile these connections are. I didn't want to mess it up by being messy.

When we got to the village, I bought the chips (she tried to pay. I said no. She bought the cokes) and drove a little further, to the car park over the beach. I pulled up next to a row of camper vans and nodded to a guy in board shorts. North-coast Cornwall is good for surf, but not today. Not enough wind. The guys were out anyway, about five of them, just bobbing black dots on the swell.

We settled on the sand, close to each other but not touching. Not yet. She bumped up the distance between us. 'Do you surf?'

'When I was a lad, sure. But not much any more, what with work. These guys get up at five to come down here in the summer.' I stretched and gave a comedy yawn. 'I like my sleep.'

'Me too.' She flicked a grin at me. 'I love bedtime.'

We were doing that eye connection thing. It was exciting, that little electric trill when we peeped at each other too long. Like playing hide-and-seek. And she was pretty, I decided. Not crazy-hot, but her textures came together in a way that I found touchable. I thought about taking her hand, then remembered the advice from Kerry on reception. *Ask her about herself. Compliment something not obvious.*

'I like your trainers,' I said. 'Let's eat. Or the seagulls will get it all.'

'They'll be too fat to fly.'

'Like me.' I rubbed my belly. 'Must get back to the gym.'

'Oh, me too,' she said. 'Next week.'

▼

I'd been told the chips were good, and they were. Salty and thick. We munched in silence, watching the sky do its thing over the silver-flat sea, then cracked our cans and drank deeply, hiccupping and supressing belches with a hand over the mouth. Once my mouth was empty, I panicked over what to say. Ask her about work? Boring. Ask her for a kiss?

Not yet. There was about one mouthful of coke left in my can, so I sipped it, smiled at her, sipped it again.

Fuck. I was at a loss. Then a seagull swooped over our heads to land on the *car park closes at ten* sign. 'I wonder why they close the car park? It's not like you can't leave your car along the road.'

'Maybe it's a dogging spot,' she giggled. 'Too hot for the locals, so they make a rule that means someone will be along every night. Puts people off.'

'Dogging?'

'Rife round here in the summer, so my mates say. Have you seen any?'

'Saw some bouncing cars once in a layby,' I lied.

'Might have just been normal fucking.' That familiar word was somehow shocking from her, in a good way. 'Not much else to do around here when you're growing up.'

I laughed. 'Speaking from experience?'

She bit another chip, her teeth a neat row, and ignored my question. 'You know there's a code?'

'What?'

'For dogging. Signals. So, if the internal light is on it means come and watch but no touching allowed, I think. And there's something about the doors. Different doors open mean different things.' She dipped her finger in the ketchup. Licked the tip at me. 'You should look it up.'

'Maybe I will.' I took another swig of my coke. 'It's not really my thing though.'

The conversation paused again. Kerry had laughed at me when I'd asked for advice, but she hadn't told me what to do should the conversation swerve into sex so soon. I took a deep breath. 'I really like your trainers,' I said. 'Where are they from?'

'Sainsbury's.' She looked down at her feet. 'Shall we go and explore?'

We put our papers in the covered bin, the cans in the car for me to take home and recycle. The path down to the beach was bumpy but wide, and I helped her a few times, not that she needed it, but it was nice to hold her hand for a moment.

'Wish it was warm enough to go paddling.'

'You can if you like,' I replied. 'I've got towels in the car.'

'You came prepared?' she grinned at me. 'I like that. But no, let's just walk a while. I want to see what's around this way.'

The sun was setting, clouds gathering. We wandered up the beach.

'Oh, that's cool,' she said, pointing to a pile of rocks under the cliff. The sea had stacked them into a pile, the power of the water organising and sorting them into size. Little at the bottom, big at the top. And above all of them a boulder, about eight feet high, with a hole in the centre about two feet across, twisting up into a crack that appeared at the top. There was light inside the hole, like a mini cave, so you could tell the crack went all the way through. 'Never seen something like that before.'

'Me neither. I wonder what caused that?'

I dredged up some of my geography GCSE. 'I expect it's the sea, getting in when the tide is high and eroding it away.'

'Looks like someone drilled it. It's like a passageway.'

'Yeah.'

We moved closer. She was deft, lightly hopping from one rock to another. I was slower. By the time I reached her, she was already on her hands and knees at the lowest opening. Her head had disappeared, and I could see that her shoulders were wedged into the holed rock. 'This is a little tight,' she said, wriggling to force her way in and up. 'But I have narrow shoulders.'

'Should you do that?' I asked

'Oh, I expect it's something all the locals do round here. Probably has some quaint customs attached to it. Get through the hole and your husband will come home with a full net, that sort of thing.'

'Could be the opposite,' I said. 'Could be a curse.'

She stopped. 'What?'

I laughed. 'Oh, you know. Could be that this is an ancient place, to be respected.' I put on a scary voice. 'Whoever DARE shove themselves through this sacred hole shall leave ALL their good fortune on the other side…'

'Oh god,' she said. 'How long for?'

'For' – I thought quickly – 'half as many years as you are old.'

'Hmm.' The sounds of her shifting in the hole had ceased. 'That's a long time.'

'Yep.' I toed a broken shell, flipping it up on its jagged edge. 'Are you coming out?'

'Well I can't now, can I?' she said. 'I don't know whether to go forward or back.'

'Just come back. There's no way you'll make it all the way through, anyway. It's too tight.'

'But what if there's a curse for a half-complete journey? Like, something to punish you for giving up.' Was she beginning to cry? I could hear the thickening of her throat, the filling of her nose.

'There won't be. Don't be silly.'

'I'm not silly.' A note of temper rang through around the tears. 'Don't call me that.'

'Sorry.' I checked my phone. A message from Kerry on reception. *Hope it's going well! xx*

That was nice of her. For a moment, I wondered what she was doing. Probably at home with her boyfriend. Painting a wall. Swish, swish, then lean in for a kiss. Swish, swish, then…

I shook my head, then looked around for help. Down on the beach, a man was walking his dog, a big brown beast with a lolling tongue and fetching grin. 'Hey,' I called. 'Hey, can you come here?'

He heard me, and as he climbed up on the rock, I pulled him to one side. 'You local?'

I saw him tense. He frowned, cleared his throat. 'No. But look, mate…'

'Can you do a Cornish accent?' I interrupted.

'What?'

'Can you put on a Cornish accent and pretend to my friend that there isn't a story about this rock?'

He looked at me, looked at the rock. 'Look, fella. I don't have to pretend. I've lived here for twelve years. If there is a story, then I don't know it.'

'That's what I thought.' I stuck my hands in my pockets and gave my keys a jiggle. 'Sorry to bother you.'

'Hold on,' said the man. 'Is there a story? About this rock?'

I sighed. 'No.'

He stood back and appraised the boulder, eyes wide with interest. 'I bet there is. I bet it's called the devil's blowhole or something cool like that. I bet it's where smugglers or wreckers agreed to meet.' He took a picture of the rock, then jumped up to peer through the top hole at her. 'Hey, I'm Rob. What's it like in there?'

'Hey Rob,' she said. 'Feels okay. I thought I saw a beetle, but it was just a pebble.'

'Cool.' He shuffled forward some more, dipping his face into the shadow of the crack. 'Room for another?'

A pause. Some scuffles. A sigh. Then: 'No, I don't think so. It's pretty tight already. But there might be another boulder further up. We started at the car park, so carry on the opposite way and you could be in luck.'

'Ah, I can't. On my way back now, aren't I?' Rob dropped back to the sand and whistled up his dog, who was busy dehydrating itself as it covered the boulder in piss. 'Another time for sure. Have fun, yeah?'

'Bye, Rob.' Her voice was gentle. 'Hope you find what you're looking for.'

'You, too.' He nodded at me. 'Take care.'

I watched him and his dog wander back across the sand. 'Nice guy.'

'Yeah. Has he gone?'

'He's gone.' A gull swooped overhead. 'So, are you coming out now?'

'I'm actually good,' she called back. 'You don't have to wait.'

Another gull, this time with a scream so hellish it made me shiver. 'I can't leave you here. How will you get home?'

A few more kicks. 'Don't worry about that. As long as I stay here, I'll be just fine.' A shower of sand. 'I expect I'll be here for a while.'

▼

She wasn't joking. I sat by the rock for two more hours, feeling hopeless. Our conversation faltered from lack of eye contact or common feeling, especially when it came to made-up rules about rocks. At least it wasn't raining.

As the sun set and the night clouds gathered, I watched the surfers paddle their way in, to trudge up to the car park and shell themselves like runner beans. Music throbbed in the air, heavy bass that carried down to beach level where I waited, alone. The gulls were doing their job, cleaning the beach of sandwich crusts and cigarette butts, chasing each other away with flurries of wings and bad-tempered yelling.

When the last car left the car park to wind, lights on, along the coast road, I gave in, and moved out of earshot to call the police non-emergency line. Once I'd told them a woman was stuck in the rock, the operator scolded me for not calling the fire brigade. I tried my best to explain. 'Just send someone to talk to her,' I said, quietly. 'Someone with authority.'

▼

Behind and above, I could see the police car snaking along the coast road, despite the lack of flashing lights. The policeman – all chest, like a wardrobe with legs – crunched his way over to us, and seemed to grasp what was happening with impressive speed. With a tight smile, he asked me to step away from the rock so he could have a quick chat with the young lady.

I took a picture of a gull. I took a picture of a shell.

The policeman returned. 'Appears that she's wedged tight.'

'She's not. She's just pretending.' I rubbed a hand over my face. 'Are you Cornish?'

A nod.

'Great. So, do you know about this rock?'

Another nod. 'Been here longer than me.'

'I mean, do you know how she can get out?'

'She can only come out the way she went in, sir.'

'Because of the luck?'

He stared at me. 'Because the hole gets tighter the further you go. I doubt my nine-year-old could fit, to be honest with you. She won't be able to do it.'

'I will,' came the muffled voice from the rock. 'I'm inching.'

'Hear that?' I asked. 'She's inching.' I looked down at her trainers. 'She said earlier that she has narrow shoulders.'

'That's good,' said the policeman. 'We don't want her wedged any more.'

'But she isn't wedged,' I said. 'Look, can't we just grab her legs and drag her out? I suppose it isn't assault if the police do it.'

His gaze frisked me, heavy and sure. 'Listen carefully, sir. She says that her neck is stuck at an angle. If we yank her out, we could *severely* injure her.'

'Hmm,' I said. 'And I suppose we can't have that.'

'No, sir. Of course not.'

'Okay. Can I have a word with her alone?'

Nodding, he stepped away and I poked my head inside the hole. 'Hey,' I called. 'Can I ask you something?'

'Sure,' she replied cheerfully.

'Is your neck stuck?'

'No. I just said that so he wouldn't pull me out. I just can't risk it.'

'I see.' I thought for a moment, and then said, 'Can I ask you something else?'

'Hmm?'

'What's the plan? I mean, you have to come out some time. You can't stay here all your life.'

'I could. It's quite comfy, really.'

'But it's getting dark.'

'Yeah, I suppose it is. Don't you have a torch in the car? Alongside your towels?'

I did. A wind-up one my dad had given me a few years ago. 'Sorry, no.'

'Oh well. I can sleep through the dark and wake up with the sun. You know, like when you go camping. I love that.' She shifted about some more, scattering sand out of her hole and over my shoes. 'Did you read that article about how wild living can help with depression? Artificial light has a lot to answer for.'

'Yes, I've heard that.' I brushed the sand from my shoes. 'I try to stay off my phone for an hour before sleep.'

'My phone is in my back pocket. If I can reach it, it will solve my problems. I don't have a signal here, but I've got some Netflix downloads. I'll be okay for the night.'

The policeman had stepped closer and heard the end of this. 'No need for that, miss,' he called. 'I've just radioed for the fire brigade. We'll have you out quick as a flash.'

A pause. A scratching sound. Then she said, 'How long till they get here?'

'Not too long,' he said, soothingly. 'Not long at all.'

'Hang on.' With a swift twist and a kick, she was out of the hole, rolling her shoulders and taking a quick stretch before dropping onto the rocks behind us. 'Don't look at me a sec,' she called breathlessly. 'Need a quick wee and I'll be right back.' Half-running, she headed to the boulders to the bottom of the cliff, ducked down and disappeared.

The policeman stared after her, then turned to me, open-mouthed.

I couldn't help it. I laughed.

▼

By the time she returned, smiling sheepishly and tugging her skirt down at the back, the fire engine had been cancelled. When she tried to get back in the hole, I grabbed her by the wrists and pulled her towards me. 'Oh no you don't,' I said. 'This thing you're worried about, this rule or whatever, you've broken it already. Don't you see that?'

'Not at all.' She twisted from my grip, stepped back and set her hands on her hips. 'That clearly doesn't count.'

'What? Who said?'

'It's obvious. Everyone needs to have a wee. Don't be silly. Now let me back in.'

'I don't think that's a good idea, miss,' interrupted the policeman. 'Seeing as you're out now. Why don't you and your boyfriend go and get a cuppa or something?'

'No.' She threw off our hands and dived head first towards the entry hole.

'Oh no you don't,' began the policeman, catching her around the ankles. And that's when she started screaming. And I mean *screaming*. It was like something from a horror film, high and keening. I felt my teeth vibrate.

The policeman clapped his palms over his ears before turning to me. 'Look,' he mouthed, 'she's not breaking any laws here. Better let her go.'

So we did.

And in she went.

In the sudden quiet, the policeman man spat on the rock, then dragged the toe of his boot through the lumpy green mess. 'Ah well,' he said. 'I'm off shift and after my dinner. Good luck with that one. Remember the car park closes at ten.'

'Oh yes,' came the voice from the hole. 'I'd forgotten.' Another scrape, some more shuffling. 'I'll come out just before. Is that okay?'

'That's fine.' I waved the policeman off, then pulled out my phone and began taking pictures of her legs. 'You've got about forty minutes.'

'Well, we can get to know a bit more about each other in that time.' The breeze was blowing her skirt up. She had good calves, brown and strong.

LIMITATIONS

You're not a bad man. You're full of potential. There are moments when you feel like you have a power inside, that with each cell-border flex or capillary pulse the universe finds its permission to be real. There are orange lights in the distance. There is petrol in the car.

But don't sink into these connections. Instead, think about seeing her again, how wet she gets. Use the memory of those sky-reflecting eyes to trigger strong pulses. You have the potential to bring the ocean under control. You could teach clouds how to fill and gather.

Perhaps, with this one, you can finally be sated. Keep at the brim. Find some peace.

▼

Pull back and readjust. It's not working, because you are not a cloud, an ocean. She has ordered a lemonade and you were hoping for something warmer, perhaps leading to a tipsy kiss in this busy-cornered place.

Hold your focus. Nothing is happening, but that's fine. Remember this is a numbers game, where the left hand holds the promise. Think engagement rings. Or don't. Just keep your eyes limited to one side of the page, and always remember how equations love to be filled, to balance like flowerpots on a windowsill – and with just as much tragedy if you make a mistake. Broken heads for the baby walkers, pushchairs in the road.

Gravity helps. Gravity is another of your pulse-gifts to the universe, as are mass and acceleration. Apply them all here, because water isn't working. Just bend your head to glance down her dress. Understand why she is wearing a black lace push-up. She has weight and direction, knows which way to go when walking to the ladies.

You could be like her and keep your promises. Be a body made of water, a mindful mass accepting flow across equations, balancing in heels, left to right, waiting to dance, prettily impatient with potential.

▼

You're not a bad man. In all probability, you would be an excellent man, if not for the transfer of expectation. Potential is, after all, a map with an x, bringing its myth of golden chain mail, links of gleaming connection, heat-hammered and worn by warrior horses. Or so they say.

But once you set out to dig you invite disappointment, chances of cave-ins or theft, of someone else getting hurt, which is unacceptable. You know this is your last opportunity to be a good man, so message her back about Saturday's walk.

Sit on the plan. Examine the markings daily, if you must, but then replace the map under the cushion, its existence pushed to the back of your mind. You don't need another action. You can let the horses sleep for a few centuries more, far over in their left-hand field.

You're not a bad man. Between the moments you must control the universe, you are capable of giving pleasure, perhaps chasing with a dropped glove, or offering a hand for a pushchair on the bus. You can admire the flowerpots, the horses. There is petrol in the car, and yes, before you turn the key you sit there and consider potential, but isn't that enough? It's not like you imagine a spark, or dream about some hose-tip match giving permission to the universe.

You are doing everything right. Keep contained, like a potted plant, a paddocked horse. Be a buried cavern, cool and damp, where soft-slither shapes and scuttlers escape the desert's fire.

You're not a bad man, but the snip of her lighter made you want to slap her face. It was easy to sit upon this potential. She might cry, and such small water won't do any good when there is petrol in the car, pushchairs in the road.

You need a new expression.

She is sitting to your left. The smoke from her cigarette turns the air into a ruined mesh, bringing the taste of chemical consumption into your mouth. There is still some heat among the embers. You push your finger into the wet hole between her lips. It's warm in there, but, you decide, not enough potential.

She crushes out her cigarette, leans in for a kiss. Her mouth is a flower. If you had hit her, she would now be wearing your bloom upon her cheek. Perhaps blood, if you had caught her teeth. When you touch her tongue with yours, she shivers, and again you want to strike her, but what would be the point? Only your bruises have power, can serve as the entry point for some new universe. Everyone else is just darkness, waiting for permission to be real.

▼

You're not a bad man, but you're a bad man sometimes. The firework through the letterbox. The petrol from the car, inflaming. This was always going to happen.

In one explosive moment the universe forces you into being, where pulsing cells breach the borders of capillaries. It's not your fault. No one mentioned that equations sometimes work in this direction or explained that what gets pumped in can be syphoned out.

There is some pity for small water and regret for a limited bloom, but it's not the end of the universe. Skin was only made to feel. In the end, she wasn't so hot. Wasn't too wet to burn.

FREE
BODY
DIAGRAM

Because I am stupid.

Because I like to be in balance with some risk of scarring.

I hitchhike to wherever and back every Wednesday night. Each time I wear my pink hoodie from Bath Spa (*2009 Paris Survivors!*), so that my body, found in some ditch, mudded and cut, will be easier to trace.

Because they might find me naked, I also write my name along the inside of my elbow in pricked red letters. The pathologist would spot these as he inched his light across skin blackened by fist impact, rope pinch, belt beat. Perhaps strangled by hand, or with my own hair, which is just long enough. I know this because I've tried.

Of course, the flesh-writing is tenuous. I might be burnt to ash or eaten by pigs. I'd like to watermark my bones, but can't think how to manage radiation or insert microchips. But I'll get there in the end. I will be a fast turnaround, between their sandwich bites, emails, detachment. An apology for my foolishness. For taking such a risk.

▼

The first car to stop was dirty red, the driver so very old. As I opened the door, the action illuminated his pullover, irregular swirls of primary colours. How could I be scared of this? A run-over paint box. An off-duty clown.

The engine was quiet yet throaty. His hair thin. 'Got any bags?'

'Only one.' I showed him my stripy tote, name and address sewn, discreetly, into the lining. 'You going far?'

'Up the line some.'

I was already in, buckling the belt. My ride clicked his tongue, as though urging on a horse, and then said, 'So. How long've I got you for?'

'I'm not sure.' My phone was flashing. 'Let's find out.'

▼

Because I am lonely.

Because worst cases are statistically more unlikely than best-plus-fine-plus-I-can-cope.

Because I want and because everyone else wants their wants met.

I joined an online dating site. The profile I wrote is measured and playful in turns. It offers some superficial insights into my character (*well-travelled; novel reader; nail varnish addict heh*) with a hopefully judicious use of emoticons, smiling and winking as I welcome, encourage, dissuade.

My profile picture is from the Christmas party. A glass of fizz, a half-smile in my blue dress. I've tweaked it, of course, with a filter which makes my eyes alien-blue but my body, when scrutinised in this dimension, appears more or less accurate in its curves and flounces. I want these lines evinced, not outlined. Someone once said I'm a better-in-the-flesh girl, and flesh is all I have, really. When you get down to the meat.

▼

Because I am often smaller.

Because I cannot punch without breaking knuckles.

I do this when running in the woods. The track is narrow, mudded and tyre torn, with hopping-stones and roots that ask for leaping. When he comes, (and there is always a he-who-comes), we will exchange a lip curl, a nod, and I'll run on, bassline pounding in my headphones, curtailing the animal sense that manifests in pricklespine and hairline creeping. Then, six to eight paces on, I do it, that thing, that action, the same quick-flick, behind-you check cyclists are taught for when they change lanes: the lifesaver glance.

And because I am stupid – repeat-it: stupid – the one time I should have kept running I stopped. Turned back. Because he had also stopped. Had something metal in his hand, half-hidden up his sleeve.

I removed one of my earbuds. Snapped at him. 'What've you got there?'

He showed me. Long blades. Red handles. Scissors.

I nodded and ran on without running away. I'd actually wanted to wait, to give him time to speak, to describe what was happening so I could process the silver flash, the handle colour. Weigh up the best outcome. We'd needed to connect more, perhaps some light chat about possibilities. I wanted to know where the knife was. Keep my eye on the prize.

I've since worked out he was stealing holly to make Christmas wreaths. Because it must have been winter. I remember thinking my fingerless gloves would have helped me grab at the blade. And it must have confused him. Maybe he went home and told his wife about the strange woman in the wood. How she had frightened him with her pounding approach, her holly-sharp question. Her lip-curled hello and goodbye.

▼

Coffee with KrunchyPB001 was going well. He had bright teeth, clean nails, and hadn't spat his cake into my hair or mentioned a 'Muslim crisis'. As for me, I was soon doing that leg-curl thing – part bent up, part tucked under – that's been my body's way of signalling attraction since I was fifteen. I tilted my head. Pushed back my hair.

Because it doesn't matter what we are talking about as long as it is not disagreeable. I can keep going for hours in the vein of light interest, gentle mockery. The drier spots of my life's stepping stones are pointed out. The murky, stickleback-nibbled depths are not. Because we are trying to impress. Because we have the right to edit our pasts. Because not everything that I have done, or had done to me, is relevant to the person I am at this moment, leg-curled in a coffee shop.

I tune back in: 'So it's been about three years now, and I'm still as keen. Getting better all the time.'

Some sporting pursuit. A clean kit for Thursday nights. A pint with the lads. Etcetera.

'And I stopped using the books and just chuck it all in now. I'm well known for it. Expensive knives. Coriander.'

Some cookery skills. An interest to be shared. Pride in preparation. Etcetera.

Because it's all just health (exercise, good food) and confidence (education, job) but never the moments written in tiny letters, redly, on the inside of a limb. He, whoever he is at this point, will pay for our coffees and I will pay for our next. He will demur. Someone will concede. And our secret information remains covered.

This is the definition of politeness.

Because this isn't meant to hurt.

▼

It was my first lorry. Long distance driver, typically tubby but sweet-smelling. A picture of a horse in a silver frame on the dashboard. Loose hands on the wheel, loose questions to pass the time. I'd climbed three steps to enter his kingdom. It made me feel safe.

'Music?' He stabbed a finger at the stereo, and I saw a cut on the back of his hand, raised like a cat-scratch. 'You pick.'

I fiddled with buttons, but didn't press anything. 'What do you like?'

'Everything.'

A nothing reply, coffee-tongue worthy. There was no coffee here. 'Do you really like everything?'

'Prefer the quiet, truth be told.'

'Yeah.' I got that. I really did. A smooth rumble massaged my bones. It would have been a shame to hide it under beats and the failings of a flawed lyric. 'Let's leave it off and talk.'

'What do you want to talk about?'

I leant my head back, kicked off my boots. Brought my knee up to my chest.

▼

Because he lied about signs.

Because scissors are everywhere.

Because I am free Wednesday, I decide to meet.

DarkSky00, five feet eleven, council worker, team sports and cooking. He had wanted to take me for pizza, but I never agree to mealtime durations. Exit routes need to be kept clear. After some smiley-icon lying from me he'd agreed to tea and cake, placeholder ideas that realised into a glass of wine for him and a coffee for me.

'It's not that I have anything against her. It's just she didn't tell me why.'

His marriage, ended in shattered glass and bare feet; his need to talk about it. I didn't mind. There was no harm here, in this lack of attraction. Motorbike admiration. Questions of helmet safety. A road with clear white lines to follow.

'So, I'm having fun just getting out there. What do you like to eat? Curry?'

'Well, I—'

'It's just that my ex was sensitive to spices. We ate a lot of bland food.' He had another wine. I stirred my cold coffee, thought about the phone in my pocket. Plenty More Men, tapping at the glass. They have eclectic taste in music. They like my pics, my pix, my picks.

I brought my cup to my lips, poked my tongue into the settled dregs. I thought it'd be bitter, but it wasn't that bad.

'Do you want another?'

'Oh no, thank you. I'll be climbing the walls. Shall we go?'

Cheeks pink and lightly sweating. Tight tuck of shoulders as he slid the leather back on. Bent for a kiss. Took two.

I used to pat these men on the arm when I said goodbye, promising to have a think before I got in touch. I don't do that anymore – the patting, I mean. It seemed a little unkind, as I am usually writing their *but-I'll-think-you'll-agree* brush-offs in the car park. Quick and clean.

Because it won't hurt as long as I say it doesn't hurt. And that goes for them as well.

▼

Lawrence drove either a black or dark green Volkswagen. Hard to tell in the orange light, in the drizzle that made the streets shine like polished glass. As I opened the door, he was brushing the seat free of McDonald's straws and Twix wrappers, knocking them into the footwell. 'Cleaner's day off.'

I laughed. 'She's a lazy cow. She's been promising to do my kitchen floor all week.'

'Don't know why we put up with it.'

'Shall we fire her?' My boots, solid soles good for running away, for kicking at fists and faces, crunched plastic packets, found a soft something that could have been the crust of a pie.

'Perhaps.' He exhaled, and I smelt his sour-belly breath. 'But then we'd have to do it all ourselves. And we're too messy, aren't we? We sleep in dirty sheets.'

▼

I wore a different dress when I met HolderPZ, one that slipped from the shoulder and showed my bra strap. I hiked it up, said hello, wondered aloud about the merits of the long black over the americano, and for five minutes he wouldn't meet my eyes. I wasn't bothered. I'd had shaky-hand starers, dribble-lip coughers, open-mouthed mannequins and tight-smile haters. He'd settle down.

In the meantime, I made the most of looking. A lithe man in a heavy cotton shirt, expertly pressed. Light eyes that trickled over my body then slid to the corners of the room. A watcher, then. A weigher. Maybe money, maybe not, but a whiff of status – that confidence that comes with good shoes. When we finally, fully looked at each other, something hiccupped in my gut.

'Now, how's the dating treating you?' This as he picked out a brown sugar lump from the bowl. 'Are you having fun?'

'Everyone's been very nice. But, you know.'

'Yes. Sometimes I think we're in a holding pattern.' He crunched the sugar between his front teeth, gave a granulated smile, then found a way to compliment my hair.

I bought the second coffee and started my routine – hobbies to siblings to taste in film – but he wouldn't let me lead, wanted to know about me. Answers led to more questions, and I became aware of a version of myself manifesting between us. She was a big-smiler, socially alive, sexually assured, and her skin was covered in red letters, descriptions of what she did for work, her home routines and thought patterns. How living alone pleases. Favourite drink, best name for a dog if she owned one. All of those individualities. She was colouring herself in, arms up over her head as though being stroked, being undressed.

'I'm so sorry,' he said, 'I have to take this call.' He patted my arm. 'Shall we have a think and message?'

▼

Sandy didn't know it, but he was taking me home. I'd mentioned meeting friends at The Harvester, as I could walk it once he'd pulled away, probably giving that two-beep salute that makes me wince as it wakes the neighbourhood babies – but for now he was happy prattling, making a life for me out of his own impressions, his resonant experiences.

'I expect you're one of them artists, aren't you? Pulling plastic bottles out of the recycling and making puppets with them.'

'No, I—'

'I knew a girl who use to do that. She ended up on heroin and her feet smelt so bad they wouldn't see her in the bank. Kicked her out.'

'That's very sa—'

'That's what you get when you don't pay your council tax.'

After this Sandy lost me, somewhere in the rumblings of his stomach (skipped his tea for me, didn't he) and the mutterings into his not-sandy beard. The white lines were yellowing. The edges overgrown and blurred by shadows.

'You're a beautiful girl,' he said at last. 'You shouldn't be doing this on your own. Where's your boyfriend?'

A breath like running in the woods. 'I don't have one.'

'No?' He rubbed at his hairy chin, sending white flakes into the space between us. 'Why not?'

Because we are not afraid of scissors, and because sometimes we tell the truth, but mostly because he asked,

I told him, Sandy-with-the-dark-hair, that I break the skin on the inside of my elbow with the tines of a fork. That I am allergic to kissing. Then Sandy told me about the woman he'd left, her addict life too much, in the end, even through her sobriety. He described her monthly sorrow, the lining up of eggs in the morning, hoping they wouldn't roll from the counter before she'd dipped them in the sink. 'Floating is bad,' he said. 'Like for them witches.'

Then we had to stop because of workmen building a roundabout. Their hi-vis coats shot laser beams. Sandy dipped his lights. 'Not much left to do now, surely. Been going on for months.'

'More like years.' I picked up my bag from the floor. My phone was glowing. 'But there's always something else.'

The Harvester windows were dark, the bar obviously closed, so Sandy insisted on dropping me at my door. 'Not safe for young ladies,' he'd said. 'Never forgive myself.'

He didn't double-toot; must have known I wouldn't like it. We'd talked about the quiet, about hiding in houses, about living alone. Waiting for something to happen.

Because it goes like this: double unlock, kitchen light, glass for wine, knife for cheese. Kick off firm-soled boots, check dating app.

Tap, tap on the glass. *Tap tap.* Let me in.

Over the shoulder, a lifesaver glance.

Because he's there.

MOMENTUM

I was downstairs when my phone buzzed, the email showing my name next to Dilly's on the helper list. After a swift victory lap of the kitchen – sunflower tea towel my winner's flag – I showed Mum, who pinched her mouth up and said, 'You're forbidden to get in his car.'

Every grown-up says this whenever Dilly's mentioned. It used to frighten me when I was little – like, exactly what was he going to do to me in there? Chop me up, or do some weird paedo stuff that no one would explain? Now I'm older, I reckon it's cruel. My teachers would call that bullying, would ask *who doesn't make mistakes? Are you perfect?*

'Blah blah.' I flopped back into my chair to fiddle with the salt and pepper. 'That happened before I was even born.'

'So?' She'd moved behind me, slamming drawers and slicing bread. 'I'm giving you tomato. And don't say blah blah.'

Eye-roll. 'Not as if anyone died.'

The knife clattered on the counter. 'No excuse. His poor

wife must have been terrified. Drunk-driving with his kid in the car? No thank you.' She dropped my plate in front of me, then touched my head as she turned away. 'I don't blame her for taking off. If your father had ever…'

Mum didn't finish this thought, probably because Dad hadn't been a drinker and anyway, he's not around to leave. My stomach pinched. I'd hate for her to think about that time. I gulped my coke, jiggled my belly and let rip a mighty burp so she'd tell me off for being gross.

Mum knows my tricks. She slid in next to me at the table to pick dead petals off the plants. 'Sandwich nice?'

I made a *mmmmmm* sound.

'Good. As for Saturday, what happened to running the cakes? I was hoping for some cheap lemon drizzle.' A short pull, a twist, and another flower gone. 'Never thought you'd be with that man.'

'Yeah.' I bit into my sandwich again, cucumber firm against my teeth.

I'd made a point of asking to be Dilly's assistant. Three years I've been helping at Maynard's Day, and three times I've ended up on some shitty stall, running the tombola or selling piles of broken crap. It's *boring*. Other kids my age never hang around long. They all have *much* better things to do on a Saturday in June. And though adults might talk to you for a while, they soon drift way into 'grown- up' conversations, the ones they hate you overhearing, and so I'd end up fetching endless cups of tea or patrolling the edge of the field, stuffing crisp packets and ice-cream wrappers into a carrier bag.

But Dilly didn't gossip. Dilly was cool, in his weirdy-beardy way. 'It won't be so bad,' I told her, wiping my mouth. 'And it might be fun to work on the Box for once.'

'Maybe,' said Mum, as she scooped up her pile of trimmings. 'Not sure it should be allowed, really. The fete is for raising money, doesn't he get that? He should at least charge for his… experience.'

'It's just performance art.' I'd heard someone say this once and repeating it made me feel mature. 'Some sort of theatre.' That felt close to the truth, and yet Dilly didn't seem like an actor, all wide eyes and hand movements in every interview. He was the opposite: skinny and still, with a voice that rumbled and scraped like a skateboard. Mostly he just seemed tired, yet he lived in our busy-bodied, organised little town, so every church fete, school disco, farmer's market or Halloween, Dilly would turn up in his battered old car (one red door, one gaffer-taped window), open the boot and set up the Box, tweaking lines and adjusting angles, before thumping down into his deckchair to read a book – historical romance, we'd noted, giggling – until someone came by to take the bait.

'It'll be sunny,' Mum said. 'Don't forget your cream.'

'I know.' There's no point telling her that, but I said it anyway.

'Blah, blah.' She touched my head again, hands smelling of green. 'And wear a hat, okay?'

▼

Dilly's car pulled into Maynard's Field, and he got out to say hey. I'd not seen him in months, but he looked the same: grey-headed, Gandalf beard, cut-offs and sandals, like some old hippy in an American comedy.

'You feeling strong?' he asked, giving me the once-over.

'Yep.'

'Then let's get cracking.'

We set the Box up on the edge of the path to the sunken garden; that way, most people would walk by us on the way to the main fete. The thing wasn't much to look at, truth be told, looked like a wardrobe, if you took away the doors and the back. A rectangle of thin wood covered in wires and scrunched-up tinfoil, the tiny balls glued or soldered onto the frame. Honestly, it looked a mess, like the crap little kids make for Mother's Day, smeared in glitter and badly-controlled paint.

Not that it mattered. We'd all taken our turn, no questions asked, queuing in the sun to hop, jump or cartwheel through, squealing as we tumbled into the unknown. Landing on the other side, we'd check ourselves over – fingers in ears, wiggling some odd-dimension pressure out by moving jaws up and down, patting chests and stomach – *am I here? In one piece?* – and then, confused as much as proud, we'd give the waiting kids a thumbs up. And Dilly would say it, say his line, variations of *I guess you're in the right place, kid*, or *great work, sweetheart! Now make the most of it*, which meant it was time to sip blackcurrant squash, chuck grass and run screaming from the killer wasps.

So even though Dilly was a fraud and the Box was a con, I wanted to work with him. Because us older ones, we never told. Took the little ones through it like Dilly was Santa. Building them up to their timeline jumps, encouraging daydreams of where they would end up – ponies, beaches, things like that. Kids are so sure they're special that they keep on queueing, keep trying, even when the ten kids in front had run off confused. None of them knew the term 'anti-climax' – I mean, I only learned it a year ago – but that was definitely how they felt. I know because I remember. After my jump, I'd gleefully searched for the difference, for talking dogs or flying cars, and then, remembering to check my arms, I'd seen the splodges still there, each orange bloom marking me as my father's child.

'You're in the right place,' Dilly had called. 'Be happy.'

And I kind of was, for a while, even though I knew nothing had changed.

▼

'But it doesn't make sense.' We were into our third hour, the crowd had slowed, and I was feeling brave enough to question the science. 'There's already a me on that timeline, so what happens to them?'

Dilly marked his page with a torn takeaway menu. 'Oh, they're still there. And they're you, so it don't cause problems.'

'Do you mean there's a me left here, on this one? So we've made another?'

'No, no,' he grunted, 'this ain't Star Trek, with wormholes and stuff like that. You won't get it.'

'I will if you explain it. I'm top in science.' This was a lie, but whatever.

'Top, eh? How about you get school done and dusted and *then* come back to me.' Dilly bent forward, plucked a piece of stray tinfoil from between two blades of grass and peered at it. 'Fuck,' he said. 'Hope this didn't drop off the rear quarter.'

'What happens if it did?' I asked, taking a look.

'Oh, I don't like to think about that. Too depressing.'

Dilly slipped the scrap of metal into his pocket. 'Hasn't gone wrong yet, put it that way.'

Hasn't worked, either, I began to say, biting it back just in time. No need to make things awkward. Instead, I pulled out my phone, stretched out on the grass. Everyone else had gone into town, meeting up in Burger King, and I wanted to see what was happening. And then one of the little kids from the houses at the back of the park – I don't know his name, but I know his cousin from karate – marched right up to Dilly and kicked him on his bare ankle. And I mean *hard*.

Dilly shot out of his chair, slapping at his leg as though a bee had got him, then stood over the boy. I was already at his side, taking in the boy's puffy face, the bottom lip wobbling and ready to wail. He showed us what was cupped in his hands: a tabby kitten, small, pink-nosed and dead.

'Send her through,' ordered the boy. 'Send her through the Box. Right now.'

The man sighed. 'I can't do that, my friend.'

'Send her through.' The boy's face crumpled. 'Please, Dilly.'

Dilly peered at him. 'Been though yourself?'

A nod. 'Ages ago. When Cally Woodruff rode that horse.'

'So, you know you're on the best line for you?'

The boy nodded again, so hard that he lost his footing, almost falling until Dilly put a hand on his shoulder.

'And you understand that, if we send her through, you won't see her no more? That this line's done for her?'

'I get how it works,' he said, scowling. 'Just make her better.'

'So give her here.' Dilly took the scrap of fur carefully in a cradle made of both palms, and blew over her peachy fur. 'She was a pretty one,' he murmured. 'Bet she'll have so much fun in her new life.'

He stepped through, his back to us for a few seconds, and then came around the back to stoop and show his empty hands.

The boy reached out, hesitated, and then stroked the place where the kitten had lain. 'She's gone?'

'Yes, she's gone,' said Dilly softly. 'It's worked.'

The boy stared up at us, suddenly suspicious. 'But *where* has she gone?'

Dilly laughed. 'Cheeky bugger. You told me you knew the answer to that. Go home, now. Tell your mum what happened.' He met my eyes. 'Tell her to ring me if she wants.'

The boy ran off, surprisingly fast on his short legs. Relief, maybe. I watched him disappear behind the tea tent.

'Oh, hey,' I said. 'That was weird.'

'Hope he doesn't go telling all the other kids.' Dilly stuck his hands in his pockets and gazed after the boy. 'I don't need a trade in dead pets. Or family members.' He snorted. 'I can see it now – some lady demanding I take grandpa's coffin through.' He shook his head, beard waggling, and turned to unclip the Box's sides. 'Though, I'm surprised it's taken this long for someone to ask.'

There was a pause. It stretched out like elastic, like chewing gum pulled from between the teeth. 'No one's going to bring you a dead body to put through,' I said, eventually. 'That's just sick.'

'Yep.' The Box was nearly down, plywood bowing as we shifted the sides apart. 'But people are sick. Think about it.'

I stared at him. Somewhere up his sleeve, or wedged in his skinny armpit, a dead kitten wasn't thinking about anything. I held out my hand. 'You did your part. Give me the kitten and I'll bury it under the trees when no one's looking.'

'No kitten here,' he said, snapping the deckchair shut. 'She's off somewhere else now, sucking on her mum like nobody's business.' He looked at me from the corner of his eye. 'Which it ain't.'

I blushed a little at that, but soon shrugged the weirdness off and helped him pack up. We collapsed the joints, folded the crumbling foils, chips of silver paint sticking to my palms. The other stallholders had marked down their Victoria sponges, yelling out deals on their muddy leeks, but the Box had shut up shop.

'Time for a pint,' said Dilly, opening the car door. 'Coming?'

WITH
COMPLIMENTS

We are the hotel of the lost. There are no maps on the front desk, because none of you would read them. There isn't a street sign on the wall outside. The door has no number. You found us anyway. Welcome.

Sinead has been running. Two minutes late is okay. Five is a problem. She is at eight minutes past the hour, and auditions are rare, bar jobs inflexible, but she is here now. No spotlight. No curtain. Four boxes on the stage. One dressmaker's dummy peeking from the wings. The sleeping hush of a theatre in the daylight. The lights up, showing the gaffer-taped marks, the cable ties. She can breathe. Everything is fine.

Marco strides up to give her quick hug, half-pulling her over the front row seats. 'Glad you could make it, darling. Freddie's out, but we've roped in Paul to read. He's marvellous. Such a generous presence.' His eyes are actually wet. 'We all love Paul.'

Sinead was sweating in her tight top. The theatre was dusty-cool. 'I've run over it a few times now. It was so good of you to think of me.'

The last time she had seen Marco he had been shoving her out of his front door at six in the morning, her good shoes in her hand. *Marvellous, darling,* he'd said then, too.

'Well we are always looking for the next breakthrough and have heard good things. We're on a schedule so are you ready? Paul is ready, aren't you, darling? We all love Paul.'

Sinead pulls her stomach in. The test had been negative, so she'd deleted his number. Had been surprised when her agent had given her his name.

'And we must go for a drink.' His eyes on her breasts. 'We'll be making up our minds for a while, but it'll be so lovely to reconnect. You must tell me everything you've been up to. I'm hearing marvellous things.'

▼

We serve porridge in the morning. We prepare you a sandwich for lunch. Evenings are baked potatoes, chips or rice, with one choice of vegetable and a protein source exactly half the size of your fist. There is no salad. There is water in plastic jugs, to be drunk with plastic beakers.

▼

Sun cream. Baseball cap. Headphones. Comedown. Connor stabs another polystyrene tray stained with mustard. Stabs another paper cup. Stabs some yellowed leaves, even though they are not really rubbish but he's *into* it now, the clearing, the sense of achievement at leaving a clean swathe behind him, marking his route through the arena where yesterday the music had given him that leg-up-and-over the wall of his mind.

There is money on the floor. The ends of joints and dropped baccy tins with sweet-pill extras. There are pairs of knickers, bandanas, flags and flip-flops. People have stumbled back to their tents one-footed, naked, cashless and kissing. They left the things for Connor to find. A treasure hunt as payment for his ticket. A lawnmower-stripe action, up and down, up and down. Putting the rubbish away.

He feels a tap on the shoulder, and he pulls out his right earphone, cocks his head.

'What do I do with the bottles full of piss?' The lad is unhappy, red-faced, no sun cream, no hat. He is stabbing wildly, without precision, without a plan.

'Just leave them there, mate,' said Dave. 'Someone will clear them up.'

'Are you sure?'

'Yes, mate.' Connor turns away, screws his headphone back in, and gets back inside the smooth beat of the morning's morning-after tunes. It's not the rush, but not quite normal. He should really eat something soon.

▼

We do not have a television. We do not have any books. There is no wifi. There is no bar.

The sound of dropped money rings through the shop. The girl with the black wayward curls has dropped her coin purse, so now there is silver, gold and copper stippling the floor, round scars like the chewing-gum-covered pavement outside. Reddening, she apologises to the checkout girl, who doesn't mind but doesn't smile. It's Saturday.

With cracking knees, the man queueing picks up as much as he can, but it's hard with his bitten nails. Here you are, he smiles. He feels good about himself, like he has done the right things, and praises himself for the good boy he is. Perhaps he will go home and tell his wife, and she will say something to annoy him, probably, her hair up in that ponytail, her little white mouth. This time he will let it go. Sit on his hands till they tingle and die.

▼

There are no expectations of conversation. If you desire morning pleasantries, please be sure to order them the night before. You will not receive them.

▼

The woman is pulling at a pasty in a greasy bag. The smell of the food makes the girl feel sick, but it's more than the eating: it's the need. With her phone away and her knees spread, the woman is looking for someone to talk to. The girl can tell, because she knows the signs: when people sit next to you at bus stops and observe you out of the corner of their eye, let you know that they know you are aware of them. They make the secret look obvious, intruding with their unobtrusiveness.

Then they will sigh, one deep, drawn-out sigh, to prepare the lungs for the pauses of speech, get vocal chords tremoring in preparation for the comments, the description, the enquiry, – whatever it will be – the words becoming an envelope, stuffed with pain and handed over.

The girl used to allow them to use her like this. She doesn't anymore because she has become too thin to take it, too weak to tear open the envelope and exclaim over its contents.

When the sigh comes, the girl is ready: she pulls out her own phone. Checks today's calorie deficit. Decides to walk home and record it as exercise. The red numbers improve her value. She will pick up stones and put them in her pocket, to let gravity help her decrease.

▼

We do have a complaints procedure. You will find paper and a pen (chained) to the shelf by the bin. Write your concerns and then place them in the bin. PLEASE NOTE: We do not allow items to be placed in the bin. Please do not write on the paper.

▼

'I was expecting you to ring first. I haven't tidied up.'

'That's okay, Nikki. You should see my house. But we are here now and just need to take a quick look at the boys, see how they are getting on in the new place.'

'Can you give me five minutes?'

'We can give you five, but then we have to come in, Nikki.'

'Wait there, then.'

His colleague shuffles his feet, muttering, 'Give her time to hide the drugs, get the boyfriend out of the window…'

He shrugs, picturing Nikki looking up at him. Kitten-small, she is too young for all those babies. Her makeup is too thick, applied like greasepaint, like playing a role, but it can't hide how pretty she is, how her skin is unmarked, unlined, no puffs or crevices of care. She grins and there is a tooth missing from the side of her mouth, but it seems charming. She talks a lot.

Inside, the house smells. There are plates in the sink. There is a spilled can of lager in the corner of the room. There is a takeaway carton with half-eaten noodles, sad grey tiny prawns, little scraps of meat and vegetables; the special-fried whatever was in the kitchen, thrown into the pan and called dinner.

Among the mess, the spilt bin bag, the children are rosy. They are clean and bright-eyed. They sit on their mother's lap and stare. They giggle at his voice, at his rolling r's when he says these words: required, removal, rehome.

In your bedroom you will find a bed for sleeping. You may occupy this space from ten to six, eleven to seven or midnight to eight. There are no other slots. There are no clocks. There is no time.

▼

It's a first kiss. Well, not really. There have been others, many others, throughout the years, with other people. It's not even the first kiss with him. There have been others there, too – precursory kisses of greeting and growing familiarity. A connection of lip to skin, not lip to lip. Then the walk to the car, the end of the evening, the dinner disappointing in its amount, its price, its flavour, its presentation, but all of that is the climb up the steps to the diving board, careful on the wet floor, knowing it is coming and hoping that it is executed well, that she remembers the right steps, when to curve, how far to leap without danger, how to not let go of the rail until that time comes.

It's a good kiss. He is no tongue-jabbing mouth-claimer, no faux-shy hesitator. There is whiskery spice-smell, clean undertones, the correct covering of teeth. There is a gentle pressure on the arms, around her back, that gets more forceful before she can pull away.

The diving board bounces. She has forgotten her training. Hopes she won't drown. Knows she will.

▼

When you leave after breakfast please remember that other guests are also leaving. Do not impede each other on the conveyor. Do not forget to keep your arms at your side, your gaze straight ahead. This helps ensure a smooth transition.

▼

Crabbs folds his flame-retardant jacket into the locker. Slams the door. 'Did you lot hear? Solomon's wife lost the baby. Sixteen weeks.'

One of the Daves sighs. Another one says, 'Oh, shit.'

'Yeah.' Crabbs shoulders his bag. 'Don't say anything, mind.'

The other Dave walks out of A-Building to the bike shed. Sees Solomon bent to undo his lock, deflated rucksack like a shell over his back. Calls over to him. 'All right, mate?'

'All right,' replies Solomon.

Dave jingles his car keys. Thinks about fitting the bike in the boot. Thinks about the pub. Sniffs around the parameters of the interaction. Wards himself off. 'Friday tomorrow.'

'Yeah.' The clunk of gears. The click-click of the chain. 'Fridays are the best. See you.'

▼

While going about your day you will not be able to speak. You will forget. Please do not worry. You will find your way back. You built this place. It is yours.

HARMLESS

SO here's something for nothing. You know those guys, the ones on the street, all *hey baby hey baby hey looking gooooooood?* Well, one got me the other day as I was walking home from college. All the usual *hey hey smile hey hey hey can you hear me* stuff.

I could hear him. He was walking in front but facing me, you know? Like he was walking backwards, little step by little tripping step, so he wasn't looking behind him, didn't see the yellow tape and then—

CRASH!

He fell into the hole.

So I was confused, yeah? I mean, he'd been trying to confuse me, like by getting too close, making my heart beat that little bit faster, you know how it is, like not knowing at what point between own-thoughts and stone-face you need to be. I SO wish I was more like Maya. She has the BEST non-face. She can look through you, like ICE COLD, like she can't hear you, or see you, but hates you anyway. Like she can smell you, and you smell bad, and you should feel ashamed.

But even if I was Maya, I might not be able to get the face right. Might flicker with the lip-twist by accident. And that's worries me, because some heyheys think that I don't know that they're not just friendly, and so – even though it's been a long day at college and I OBVIOUSLY don't feel like talking – that lip-twist somehow betrays a secret understanding, a signal that I can see into their heart and soul and whatever else and JUST KNOW that they aren't the kind of heyhey to worry about.

In fact, the lip-twist can hint that me and whoever could be lip-twist friends if they will JUST CARRY ON saying hey, because hey is ok, yeah? Because then all they want is a hey back and they aren't the ones making it awkward for everyone by being rude and anyway it's only a hey, isn't it, so where's the harm, you stuck up bitch?

Or they might tell me to smile and think that no one has ever told me to smile before, so I am not smiling not because I am sad but because I forgot to smile, which is hard to do when I'd rather be thinking about college and about whether Maya will come over tonight and what we'll eat while we watch tv.

And so yeah, it's all stuff, but the smile thing is REALLY stuff, like being ordered to be happy, just so they can see me happy. I mean I suppose it's possible that their daughters smile all the time, some genetic program or physical quirk meaning they curl their lip-sides at all times without emotion or an ache, so when their daddies see a girl with a relaxed face they get all confused and worried and squeeze out our smiles the same way they'd give the Heimlich if we'd swallowed a grape.

So yeah, there I was, *heyhey*ed and heart-beaten, working at my flicker-face stare-through smile, and suddenly he was gone, dropped through the floor. There was an alarm beeping somewhere behind me. It was pretty loud, but I still heard the crash. And it was a deep hole, yeah? It was like, I don't even know, twice the height of my dad. I went closer so I could see where he had landed, and saw him on a load of metal piping, all torn and jagged.

Hey hey hey he was saying again, but his voice had changed. Hey, can you help me? Are you okay? I leant over as far as I dared.

I've hurt my leg. It's bleeeeeeding oh god call an ambulance.

Okay. Stay there.

I don't know why I told him to stay down the hole. He wasn't going anywhere. The beeping alarm was louder, so I'd had to really shout, and then there were yellowjackets.

Hey hey, said the yellowjackets. Yellowjackets never shout, not while they are wearing their company's name on their coat. Get away from that hole, missy.

But, I said.

No buts. We're filling her up.

The truck's reverse alarm got so loud I had to cover my ears before it reached the edge of the hole. Then there was a different noise as the machinery lifted the back. And there might have been another sound, a muffled *hey* as the earth poured from the truck's tipped bed, but I wasn't sure.

I went home. Maya was already there. We had burgers. Watched CSI.

A THEORY CONCERNING LIGHT AND COLOURS

There are therefore two sorts of colours.
The one original & simple; the other compounded of these.
— Isaac Newton

British Library. Outside. You looked up. I wanted to see your mouth move, the shape of your lips under the scarf. 'Can I get a light?' I asked, and immediately shut my eyes. Should have said 'May I'. I never remember this.

All those numbers in my head.

I opened my eyes to see you holding out the lighter. Green fingerless gloves made your hands look strange, and you still hadn't said a word. Maybe you didn't speak English. I wondered what languages you spoke, then lit my cigarette, gave you back your lighter. Casual, casual. 'What you reading?'

You flipped the book up to show the cover, where a woman and a dragon fought over a child.

I didn't know anything about Blake, except, 'He made this statue of Newton, didn't he?' I pointed to the metal man on the plinth behind me, his back-breaking pose, his concentration.

'Close enough.' You weren't frowning. Not quite. 'It's from one of his pictures. Always makes me smile when I see it.'

'Yeah?' I touched the chair opposite you; decided to risk it.

'It's a joke on the scientists.' English accent, somewhere south. Bristol, I know now. 'That's not really Newton.' You sat back in your chair, pulled the scarf from your throat, and your hair swung over your shoulder. I hadn't realised how long it was; not plaited, but twisted into a shining rope, black and yet alive with light.

'I'm a scientist.'

'Are you?' You looked me over. 'What sort?'

Beside us, the weight of the metal man shifted. I started to remember magnetic forces, concentration gradients, the conduction of heat as my palms touched the freezing tabletop.

▼

Newton. The greatest influence upon theoretical physics until Einstein. This is what is says in the dictionary. I know because we looked it up.

▼

'You're a what?'

It's a word I'd never heard. When you said it you lifted your chin, but your hands were fluttering, signals of anxiety, touching your book, your teacup, as the tarpaulin flapped over our heads. 'My senses cross. Words have their own colours. Ideas, sometimes. Never numbers, though.'

I wanted to kiss you. 'Does that explain the books?'

'Perhaps. It can help me with themes, recurring ideas – like a coloured stitch on a plain cloth. It's partly conceptual.'

I wanted to kiss you more.

'Give me an example.'

You paused, holding the book up over your face. *The Moonstone*.

'When we first met, we talked about Newton. He used to be flashes of silver against maddening pink – there aren't really the words, I can't explain – but since I read about his taking over the Royal Mint his name is bright, clean gold. I can almost taste it.' You smiled into the pages, then looked up. 'Go on then, ask me.'

'Ask you what?'

'The question.'

We'd only met a few times and already you knew what I was thinking. The others in the flat-share, sleep-deprived and cliquey medical students, barely knew my name.

'Oh, all right,' I leant forward and stage-whispered around the back of my hand. 'What colour am I?'

'Well,' you said. 'It's a bit weird. I usually have colours for people. But I don't have a colour for you.'

You must have seen my face fall.

'It's a good thing. Sometimes it gets a bit much and I have to hide away.' You touch the inside of my wrist, fingers soft on my pulse point.

'Don't worry about it.'

▼

We were supposed to be studying, but I always wanted your attention. A new ploy: 'I've been reading up about your golden man.'

My desk only had one chair, but you liked to sprawl on my bed, your scuffed boots kicked off to jumble on the floor. I don't know what your essay was about, but *Lady Chatterley's Lover* was bursting with notes scrawled in lavender ink. A few escaped as you closed the book. 'Come on, teaser. Say his name.'

The great man was at the top of my playlist. It was tricky, keeping all the colours in my mind. Sometimes I'd mention something – a place name from back home, a physics term – and I could see you roll the word around on your mind's tongue and taste – what? Micro-gestures of disgust flickered like moth wings. But I could always use this other man to bring you back to me.

'I'm not sure you deserve it. How many chapters have you read?'

'Three.'

I raised an eyebrow. 'Very well.' Big breath, deep drawl. 'Newton. Newton. Newton.'

You wriggled with suppressed laughter, catching the blankets under your heels. 'Now tell me what you found out.'

'At the time, we didn't know whether colour was part of an object, or something our mind projects onto a colourless universe. Thus he performed experiments.' I closed the laptop, and picked up a pencil. 'He even experimented on himself.'

'Did he? Like a properly mad scientist?'

'Yeah.' I crept onto the bed, close enough to catch the vanilla scent of your hair. 'He shoved a stick between his eye and socket to see if that changed what he saw.' Gently, I pushed you backwards, showed you my bodkin, the end chewed and splintered. I touched your cheek with the point. 'Now, young lady,' I said, in my best mad-scientist voice. 'Would you like to repeat the test?'

You laughed, head back into the pillow as you play-struggled. 'Oh, Isaac,' you said. 'Not again.'

▼

Reviewing what I have written, I see the discourse itself will lead to diverse experiments sufficient for its examination. And therefore, I shall not trouble you farther than to describe one of those which I have already insinuated.

▼

The snow refused to settle for Christmas, which made everything a little sadder. When Dr Perl asked me if I was going home, I said yes, and he wished me a safe trip, but in reality I hadn't spoken with dad since he'd demanded my keys. I'd tried to ring a few times, but the line wouldn't connect. He'd probably cut it off, now we didn't need it for the hospital.

All my flatmates disappeared, and you came over often. The street's assault on your senses – frenzied shoppers, winter tourists, riots of language – brought you, dazed and panting, to my door. I'd lead you in, seat you at the kitchen table and soothe you with my work, reading out lists of calculations. You'd put the hood of your cardigan up over your face and lean into my shoulder. I think sometimes you slept, but I carried on with the numbers anyway; a mesh of mathematics to hold you.

When you'd calmed, and warmed, and begun to mutter about the outside world, I made you mint tea with three sugars.

'Why don't numbers have colours for you?' I'd been reading up again. 'That's how most people's synaesthesia presents. That, and colours for days of the week.'

You were pulling your hair back into a ponytail, both arms up to the back of your head, but still managed to shrug.

I was not to be put off. 'Have you seen someone? A psychologist? I expect they'd like to study you.'

That flattening of the top lip, that movement of the tongue. I'd said something wrong but didn't know what. Maybe it was the word 'psychologist.' I made a mental note not to use it again, and picked up the kettle, my hands a beigey-pink against the dark kitchen counter. I ran the tap. The water was colourless.

▼

You'd invited me to St. James's Park and told me to wear a white T-shirt. I had to buy one, four pounds, a little too tight, and I changed as I walked past Horse Guards' Parade, shoving my old top in my rucksack.

Of course, I should have been working. It was a busy term and I had a lecture that afternoon, but I reckoned I could be a little late. Maybe you were going to paint me or have a photograph of us together. Perhaps we were signed up to a flash mob, white shirts flickering as we danced though the greening undergrowth.

I reached the side of the lake, sat on a bench and watched screaming teenagers run at each other, throwing what looked like dry poster paint. Then I saw you, right in the middle of the melee, and you shouted my name, laughing, hair down, grabbing fistfuls of coloured powder from bags at your feet and flinging them at the crowd racing around you. The air was full of colour, lit by the strobes of a hundred cameras as faces, arms, and once-white T-shirts were smeared in blue and gold and red.

You grabbed me, held me hard, pulled me in. I didn't know what to do, tried to ask and immediately got a mouthful of powder. My tongue was thick with ochre and ultramarine. It filled my nose and leaked down my throat, and the burning bubbling of my belly was something like the colours of childhood, mum and dad holding each other, holding me, and it *was at first a very pleasing divertissement to view the vivid & intense colours produced thereby; but after applying myself to consider them more circumspectly,* you took my arm and spun me round, our feet clumping on the hard mud.

I got in with the boys. We were a bit rougher, only just, no harm meant; a bit of hugging, a little tripping, white teeth against a maroon face, and always the open mouth, the laughter, the sudden bent-over fits of joy.

At last, exhausted, we collapsed onto the stained grass. Our bodies were unrecognisable; altered images, modern art. The audience wandered away.

'Was that religious?' I asked as you leant over to kiss me, indigo lips on a scarlet face. I didn't go to my lecture.

▼

His name is Ashley. Even I can see that name, pale and dangerous as the smoke from my cigarette. He's studying at your university, and was at our usual table when I arrived. 'I agree with you,' he was saying. 'Blake was against Newton, thought he'd missed the whole point by concentrating on the vegetative eye.' I watched Ashley touch your elbow, fingers lingering on your skin.

'Vegetative?' I fumbled myself another roll-up. 'As opposed to the what?' I want to change the subject, to steer him away from saying Newton, made somehow worse by the shafts of sunlight falling across his lips.

'The spiritual. Blake had visions, you know.'

I didn't know that, but I was familiar with your impatience with those who claimed special access to the divine.

'You mean he was nuts?'

Ashley rolled his eyes, comically, and poked you in the ribs. 'These scientists,' he said. 'What can you do with minds like that? Trains on tracks.'

'Yeah.' That was from you. I knew you were joking, but I couldn't stop myself: the word hung in the air behind your head, brightly lit by the flame of my temper.

▼

'It's not catching,' you said later. I hadn't meant to slam my front door, but I'd been distracted by the brown envelope from the university that was hanging from the letterbox. I brought it into my room and tucked it, unopened, next to the others.

'How do we know that? It might be the side effect of a virus we can't detect. Our brains might be mixing up colours and words because they're damaged.'

'I don't have a virus.' You'd taken off your jacket and thrown it on my bed, but now you picked it up again. 'Or maybe I do. I'm not feeling well.'

You wouldn't let me walk you to the bus stop. My eyes were aching. I felt the urge to close the curtains, block the light from under the door. Something was almost snapped, half-broken; a mental limp or blister that could heal itself if I just stayed still. But every time I lay down, I could smell your hair on my pillow, that bright sunshine smell that refused to dissolve itself into chemical components: sodium benzoate, cetrimonium chloride, the explosion of hydrogen a million miles away.

I rang you but your phone was off. I left a message. You didn't ring me back.

▼

I handed in my project on Wednesday, and on Friday received an email from Dr Perl. I had only been to his office once before, on the day of my interview, and it hadn't changed much during the months between; still cluttered, dusty and smelling of burnt toast. Dr Perl shook my hand, offered me tea, and then told me that I wasn't in trouble.

'I'm sure it's a marvellous joke, and it must have taken you ages.' He handed me my project folder. 'I particularly liked the bits about the girl at the British Library. Points for making me smile, at least.'

I looked down at the sheaf of papers he handed me. My folder. My handwriting, but instead of my work it was something about light and colour.

Dr Perl took a noisy slurp of his tea. 'If it were up to me, I'd give you top marks for the hell of it, but the department has its own hoops to jump through.'

Deep dark red. Willow green. 'I didn't write this.'

'Well, not all of it. Newton lacked your turn of phrase. What was it? Something about eating paint and having a "bubbling bellyful of joy"? You should write greeting cards. Anyway, I'll give you a few days. Dying relative, ended relationship, depression, something like that should do the trick.'

He almost patted me on the shoulder when I said goodbye.

I have until Monday to give him my work. I can't explain. The words are the wrong colour.

▼

I followed you and Ashley to the cinema, so I suppose I have at least three hours. If you stay overnight at his flat, I'll have even longer. I'm not worried; I'm good at waiting. I've spent the last three days in darkness, as much as I could. Total blackness in my room, sunglasses in the kitchen and bathroom, lights off. It's been hard but I feel better; some of the visions helped me decide what to do.

The bags are heavy. I pick up my pace.

It's not hard to get into the house. Your bed is scattered with clothing, and I picture you trying on outfits, predicting Ashley's brain interpreting light waves absorbed or reflected into his admiring eyes. I wonder if he's realised your properties. I wonder if he's safe in the dark.

I open the first tin of paint and start in the far corner. The roller does the job well, wiping away the pale blue of your room and replacing it with yellow. I can reach the ceiling by standing on your chair, and, later, on the bed. I push the furniture back, and use the roller on your mirror, which takes a while as it keeps smearing and letting my reflection peek through. I paint the outside of your wardrobe and take a break, because the light has begun to taste like Newton.

There is someone moving in the house. I'm trying to be quiet, but you have so many trinkets, so many pictures of friends and family. I've brought fine-bristled brushes for the ornaments, your laptop's keyboard and screen. I don't have time to do all your clothes individually, so I use the wide roller, smoothing out patterns with a second coat. I cover the carpet, reaching as far under your bed as I can, and I'm worried about running out of paint but remember that it's dark under there and that *the colours of all natural bodies have no other origin than this, that they are variously qualified to reflect one sort of light in great plenty than the other.*

Finally, the whole room is done apart from the bed. I have one can left. I prise the lid up with the knife, throw paint all over your sheets, strip off my clothes and roll until I'm almost covered, then take a moment to check the hard-to-reach areas between my fingers and toes, the folds of my eyelids. The smell is dizzying. As the paint dries and cracks, a darker gold shows in the creases of my skin, and this is good, because it can be no longer disputed whether there be colours in the dark, nor whether they be the qualities of the objects we see, nor perhaps whether light be a body.

THE HIGGINS METHOD

So, this is life after. Reporters follow me in the street, stand behind me in shops, leaning in with their obvious ears. If my phone chirps the people around me flinch, watching from the corner of their eyes to see if I will take the call. The vocal peak of a sneeze or the rasp of my cough raises eyebrows, as though I should be completely silent. A ghost, a photograph. Mouthless.

They forget that sound can be a wound. Call my wordlessness *performance*, or *protest*, and write long articles in the weekend papers to call me troubled, brilliant, or both. I don't talk at all, it's true, but I squeak when I knock my toe on a chair leg; I laugh with the same abrasive tone he couldn't break me of. And when I sing, it feels like getting clean. The black moss scraped away.

Wait.

I didn't mean that last bit.

▼

The first time he broke into my flat I'd been at rehearsal. All he'd done was move the kettle, unplugging, emptying and placing it on my pillow, for me to wonder at and then ignore. But the second time I had been home, in bath-soaking, bell-ignoring bliss, and he'd thrown his weight against the door, rushed inside to grab me, wet and bubble-skinned, slippery with fear. After allowing me to cover myself, he'd pushed up the sleeves of my robe. 'This isn't what you need,' he'd said, rubbing roughly at the letters drawn into my skin. At my ownership of sound.

Mouth closed, I nodded my head.

'No.' With his hand in my hair, he dragged me close enough to kiss. I could smell the dirt on his teeth, the desperation of his armpit. 'I am what you need. Say it.'

Mouth closed, I shook my head. *I won't give you any more words.*

The police hadn't used the flashing lights: just rushed straight in, shouting in a clear, aggressive tone to overwhelm and trigger childhood's obedience. I got down on my knees before he did, to show him I'd remembered. I was surprised he stayed so quiet, that as they took him away, he refused to shout after me. It's not as if he'd never raised his voice: in bed with fever, he'd screamed that I was an ungrateful bitch. But that was delirium, and, after all, he'd remained silent that time he'd held my hand over the kettle to teach me about glottal stops. *BuT-ter. BuT-ter.*

It stung so much, passing my flesh through heated water, not to punish, but to purge, he'd said. To make clean. And I'd almost understood; had been teetering into love with rounded tones, new dresses and good, sweet wine.

And I know it was wrong. *Not a real relationship, Eliza.* The therapists have done their work. But we did touch each other. He never put his tongue in my mouth, not like the market boys and phone-shop salesmen I had been with before, but he was interested in its movements, its rolling and flatness, its insolence and lazy days. These excited him more than the contour of my waist, curve of breasts, or any other wetness I could offer.

With blackest moss the flowerpots… again. Again. Again.

▼

Let me try again. Words live in the air, not spelt out in their school uniforms or passport photos. Real words exist only in the mouth, formed by labial touch, fricative twists, nasal constriction. Words transmute. Breath, captured life, encodes that life. But you have to get it right.

He showed me that, when he pushed my face up against the mirror, fingers tight on my cheeks, to watch the glass fog with each exhale, each restricted sob that refused to make a word.

If you can describe properly, you can feel.

People think it's the other way round. That is their ignorance and their good fortune.

Diphthongs are long vowels, sounds put together to make a new sound. The have their own symbols. There is no diphthong in the word diphthong, which always struck me as odd, but I suppose you need to be able to describe without relying on the thing you are describing, or you end up in circular logic. *I am who I am*. Amen.

▼

Once, I was unmarked, unpatterned. Then came my first foxhole tattoo, scraped into my skin at the end of our second week. He'd explained the schwa to me – that lovely natural sound, the unrestricted vowel. Made me open my throat for him. This control has helped me sing. But there is something mystical about the schwa. I think it was the first human sound heard from the first human throat and is still travelling outward from us. Not Logos, not the word-of-the-world, but a natural, unrestricted sound, before the need for interference, before we had need for more than one way to be heard.

After my lesson, I'd told him I needed to shop for a few things. Female supplies. He had smirked and handed me a fifty pound note, pink paper folded like a valentine. Listen carefully as you walk, he said. I want a full report of accents and any inflections you find odd.

I agreed, walked to the tube station noting Arabic throat-work and North American swoops, a Mancunian patter, light on the stresses. I bought tampons and shampoo that smelt of coconuts, because I knew he liked it. Then I went to the internet café and printed out the picture of the schwa.

'It's just an upside-down *e*,' said Snare. 'Are you sure you want this? People will think you're nothing more than an old raver.'

I don't remember what I said to her with my lips and teeth and tongue, but I recall how I felt later when delivering my report, handing over his change. I felt like my skin was singing.

▼

I know curtain's in an hour when my costumier arrives. The first time she saw me in my underwear she gasped, but was professional enough to cover this with a cough. Now she knows I will only wear long sleeves, and no sheer fabric. The sounds from my mouth are ticket-bought; the sounds on my skin are mine.

Only once did she hesitate, when the latest addition was bleeding through my patch. I took her fingers, squeezed them, and she bent her head and touched it to my shoulder, just for a few seconds, brow warm through cotton.

And the work is coming on. I am barely bleeding. Snare still says I should go for colour, her pink eyes fixed on my skin, telling me how the inks are so vibrant now, the technology of the colour understood much better, that violet will amaze me – but the last thing I want are violets. I'd pointed, firm-fingered, at the black ink. She'd sighed as I slipped off my blouse.

With black. With black. With blackest moss. With blackest moss. Again.

▼

When he was in hospital, he wanted me to visit. I know this because they messaged me.

How did you get this number? I typed back, fingers sticky from my breakfast orange.

He gave it to us. Will you come?

Of course, I tap back. *Tell him I'll be there soon.*

I put the phone down, washed my hands in almond soap and dressed for my afternoon rehearsal. The crowds were already milling outside the stage door, and as I strode past, smiling, I accepted their cheers. I've earned them. My singing, said one review, is *born of suffering but transcends human care.* What action of my voice this describes I am not sure, but it keeps the theatre full, with photo requests and chat show offers that I always turn down.

We finished a little early, and so I called a taxi and went for thirty minutes with Snare. She always pushes me to try for longer, and I could, easily, because I have always been good with pain, but I need to be careful. Husband my space. So I pretend discomfort, bite my lip, fix a brave – if slightly tearful – stare at the photographs that cover the walls of her Soho shop. Men whose bodies have become books of magic, nymph-women covered in leaves, flowers that bloom from thigh and bicep. The flowers are always violets. I control the urge to look away.

▼

Today, before court, we are completing the vowel chain.

'Where do we have left?' Snare's hair is whiter than ever, if that's possible, but I know it's a lie because I can see the line of darkness from her follicles as she bends over me. The pink contact lenses, too, are not her real colour. I guess her eyes to be blue.

I don't ask why, because she doesn't ask me why.

Thin-lipped, I point to my armpit.

'That is going to hurt. Are you sure?'

I nod.

'Okay.' She pulls on her mask. 'Tap me if it gets too much.'

She doesn't understand. But that's okay.

▼

There is a protocol to escape when the police have said they cannot help. That morning he made me carry his clothes to the shore, pile them up and sit with them as he swam out. *Health of the body keeps a man kind*, he said, trunks slipping down over his hairy belly. When I saw his arm poke out of the water as he struck out, I wondered at my preparation. The extra shake of salt on his morning eggs, the secret sugar in his tea. Maybe he'd cramp, maybe he wouldn't.

Two women and a man, in red hats, just like they said. *This is your moment*, they told me. *We just walk away*.

The clothes we left on the bench for him to find, a pile of rocks weighting down his Gap jeans, Seasalt sweater. Towel folded underneath. I turned to see if he was waving but he was too far out to distinguish in the tumult of white water, and they had parked on double yellows so we had to move fast.

And it's okay to bring up Stockholm Syndrome, because there was a soft spot under my breastbone where I want him to come back, to again hold the knife against my cheek in sadness at aspirated aiches. It was structure, at least, and I had been so formless, singing into my flowers. What I will miss most, I thought, as I followed them across the sand, will be the small responsibilities, the locating of lost slippers, the preparation of evening cocoa. He liked me to sit by the side of the chair as he drank. He liked me best on my knees.

▼

Sound as a product of movement. Phrasing as a modulation of sound. Language is between the sign and signal: made with the mouth, with interrupted breath, before marks on substrate capture meaning.

Also marking a spot where something has been buried. *Go away,* or *I keep you safe,* or *be quiet now.*

▼

My barrister is fussing around me. She is worried that my written testimony might cause problems; the screen is linked to the keyboard so I can type out my answers, but as I have no medical certificate the judge might lose patience.

'It can happen.' Her lipstick is the colour of her lips, and I wonder why she bothers. 'They don't like celebrities. If they suspect you are using the court to promote yourself, it can work against you.'

I catch at the word celebrity. Is that what I am? The photographers on the steps had shot me from such close up that I had stumbled, blinded. They had shouted my name like they knew who that person was. *Eliza. Eliza.* All noise. Teeth. Tongue. Breath. The vowels sharp, the broken buzz, the gasp.

▼

At the courthouse, reporters are flocking on the steps, even though I am early. In the cool stone of the antechamber I wait for my barrister when the old, best friend finds me, hands open in that way of supplication I recognise. I made the same gesture whenever the defendant forced me to read Tennyson, tongue weighed down with stones. As if the weight of a hundred years of poetry wasn't enough.

With blackest moss…

His friend is speaking. Pleading. I shake my head.

'But look at you now, compared to where you were. Surely that counts for something?'

It does, but not in the way that he's imagining. Still, this man was always gentle. I kiss his forehead before walking away.

▼

With blackest moss the flowerpots. I never learned the rest.

COMMON CODES

For this to make sense, you need to understand that I don't wear a watch. In fact, I never wear jewellery of any kind – my dad didn't, so I don't. I never queried it. Just saw it as another passed-on prejudice, some crossed-out line on the blueprint of masculinity. Or maybe the remnants of an old spell, a practical charm, come about from noting how earrings and bracelets first weighed down the drowning boys and then ensured the corpses were rifled. Better to keep afloat, unmolested.

Anyway, watches are dated. Like lugging a typewriter around in case I want to write a letter. Which I never do, incidentally – that's what PAs are for. I send emails from my phone: a device that never leaves my person, and which also displays the – can you guess?

So yes. I don't wear a watch.

Got it? Good.

So when she slowed outside the bank, cocked her head and inquired about the time, I shouldn't have looked at my wrist, right? But I did. And not just a glance, oh no. In fact, I gave her the whole shebang. First, a hand-flick to bring up the jacket sleeve. Next, the shirt-cuff pat, two fingers only to slide the cotton aside, and then, the final move: one finger extended to tap a dial that, quite honestly, had never been borne.

And in that moment, you know what I was thinking?

Alien invasion. Don't smile.

Then I riffled through the better-educated parts of my brain, and came up with the phrase *learned behaviour*. Learned from the TV. All those old films, the black-and-whites, you know the ones. I'm no real fan, but I have seen the ones you are supposed to see, just like I've read the right books, bought the right art. And in those films, the actors, suited, smart-mouthed, are either checking watches or kissing dames.

Maybe that is what it was. She'd asked me the time, I thought about kissing her, and the two ideas had idea-babies in my head.

So yes, I was thinking about kissing her. But only idly. I am not some mad kiss-stealer, but had caught the scent of her lip gloss, some sweet fruit stickiness, and it crossed my mind that if I kissed her, I would end up sticky-sweet, and would lick my lips afterwards. I like sweet things, I reasoned, and I am hungry, and she is tall and fine.

Then I did the wristwatch routine, revealing nothing but bare-except-for-hair skin.

Crap. And she noticed, of course. She's a *noticer*.

'You forget to put your watch on?'

After a second of frantic scrabblemind to find some, any, answer, I gave a weak smile. 'Oh. Must've fallen off.'

She pursed her temptingly lacquered lips, then said, 'Expensive?'

'No. I mean. Not really.' Her brown eyes. That soft mouth. Something else was needed here. 'But it was my—' I took a mental breath. Father's? But he didn't wear a watch, as I have already mentioned, and lies can be fun, but not when they overwrite the memory of a dead parent, '—only thing I had to remember my brother by.'

The other thing you need to know is that I don't have a brother. Only two sisters, who greatly annoy me when they arrive for their once-a-year visit, and who I love madly, weeping into their shoulders before they drive away.

'I'm so sorry.' She touched my arm. 'That's terrible. When did he die?'

Now, you might think this is a bit intrusive for a stranger to ask, but my actual response was *ah, here is a woman who is good with people.* Because you know those bullshit courses? I've done them all. Good sandwiches, bad coffee, and all say the same thing. Ask questions. Give room for the answers. Ask again. Don't worry about rudeness. We all need the opportunity to speak, and, if you are a sensitive communicator (which I am, no doubt about that at all) you'll feel it when you're overstepping.

This woman, either a taught or natural emotional-water-temperature tester, was being kind. I thought about kissing her again, but only quickly. In my head she liked it and asked for more. But on the street, she was still frowning, expectant.

But I didn't feel up to murdering my new brother. 'He didn't die,' I said. 'We lost him. He went on a diving holiday, in—' (*MaliMadagascarMichigan*) '—Malaysia and, well, I suppose we just never heard from him again.' I rubbed at my (anxious) cheek, and only just avoided covering my (liar) mouth. 'He's not dead, the authorities assured us of that. Just wanted a new life. To leave us behind.'

Her eyebrows moved again – such an expressive face – and I followed her thinking. Had we, as a family, done something terrible? Was he escaping an abusive life, a brother who hated him, bullied him, perhaps, over a much-coveted-and-eventually-stolen watch? I had to fix that.

'It's not that we weren't close,' I went on, hand coming to rest over my heart. 'I love my brother. It's just that he had problems. Married very young, and she—' *(cheated)* '—died.'

Don't judge. An in-law death I could cope with.

The woman cocked her head again, but before she could enquire, oh-so-gently, about the details, I carried on speaking. 'Then the drugs, then the getting clean, and it was so hard on him. I think he'd had enough. Built a new world, beginning across the water. In the water.' Then I looked up, to stare over her head for a moment, feeling the truth of my next statement. 'He's always loved the sea.'

I sighed. She sighed. We went for coffee. I took her number. Her lip gloss tasted like cherry sweets, just like I'd thought, and when I licked my lips she laughed and said I looked like a wolf, which reminded me of a game I used to play at school.

But that was then.

▼

'Baby,' she said, standing over me. 'I have such great news.'

My back had been giving me not-so-merry hell and there is nothing that helps it more than lying on the floor. No pillow. Nothing. I need a straight line for my spine to relax into, so I can feel the nubs and sprockets clacking back into place. 'Oh yeah?'

'Yeah.' She slung her knee over me, sat astride, and then bent to put her mouth by my ear. 'I found your brother.'

'I don't have a brother.' The corona of her hair, coconut scented, concealed our faces. 'Kiss me.'

She did, then gracefully rolled off to lay at my side. 'Don't say that,' she murmured. 'You do.'

'No.'

Her fingers wrapped mine. 'You know something? I think your sadness was the reason I gave you my number. Couldn't have you lose a brother, then a watch, then get blown out by some hot stranger.'

'Who was that? Did someone walk past when we were talking?'

She play-slapped my thigh. 'Get up and get dressed. He'll be here soon.'

▼

In the shower, lathered and aching, I made a plan to deny everything. This is another strategy they teach us at work. Delete emails, shred the memos, shrug and walk away. But my brother was too alive, was part of our relationship. Also, I am not a *monster*. I felt a little bad for this real-life person, that their evening's excitement would soon be ruined by the blunt stupidity of truth. Their brother was gone, and my lie had made their pain worse.

And yet, I reasoned as I rubbed my buttocks with the towel, it didn't have to ruin the evening. We could have a meal, expressing sorrow; have a chat over rich pasta and white chocolate profiteroles. Learn about each other, and then say goodbye. I'd pick up the tab as a gesture. We could shake hands.

This was my plan, and it was good.

▼

When he arrived – when *Carl* arrived, I should say, for that was his name, and as I'd never given him one myself it seemed as good as any – with his ironed dark-blue shirt and bottle of good wine, he didn't even hesitate. 'You look the same,' he said, and there was a tear, I swear to god, rolling down his cheek. 'I've missed you so much.'

He opened his arms and stepped forward.

And that's when it happened. Felt like an alien invasion. Was probably learned behaviour. This monkey-see, monkey-do brain, this dance picker-upper, triggered muscle memory of an action I've never performed. Because he had opened his arms and stepped forward. Do you see? Can you picture this? That man, clean shirt, clean smell, white teeth, my height, was walking towards me with arms open and a tear in his eye.

And one moment I was ready with the I'm-so-sorries, and the next I was moving forward into the hug, face into his neck, fist thumping on his back, and my voice, my voice, choked small, hoarse with long-held-in weeping, muffled by skin and emotion, still spoke out loud enough for all to hear.

'Carl,' it said. 'Carl. It's you.'

ACKNOWLEDGMENTS

Grateful hugs to the editors of *Litro*, *The Manchester Review*, *matchbook*, *Neon*, *Sick Lit*, *The Stockholm Review of Literature* and *Under the Radar* for publishing my stories and nominating them for various awards. Your encouragement led to this collection. Thank you.

Delighted grins shared with Gary Budden, Kit Caless and Sanya Semakula at Influx. Your enthusiasm, skill and patience is astonishing. I'm proud to be part the gang.

Excited fist-bumps sent to CM Carter, Laura Cowan, Kristina Keliris, Aaron Kent, Rupert Loydell, Camilla Nelson, Rebecca Perl, Sophie Playle, Simon Pitt and Eley Williams. Your help is not forgotten.

Fizzing glasses clinked with my London crew. A toast to all who keep going.

Heartfelt kisses blown to my noisy readers, the likers, post-sharers and encouraging tweet-ers. You are both dark and sweet.

And a weird dance for my family, just to hear them laugh.

Love,
Annabel
London, 2019

'Payment to the Universe' first published by *matchbook*
(Pushcart nomination. Derringer Award nomination. Best Short
Fictions 2016 semi-finalist)

'Free Body Diagram' first published by *The Stockholm Review of Literature*

'Susan Frankie Marla Me' first published by *The Manchester Review*

'Exercises in Control' first published by *Under the Radar*

'Limitations' first published by *Litro*

'Harmless' first published by *Sick Lit*
(Pushcart nomination)

'With Compliments' first published by *Neon*

ABOUT THE AUTHOR

Annabel Banks is an award-winning writer of poetry and prose. Her work can be found in such places as *The Manchester Review, Litro, The Stockholm Review, Under the Radar* and *3:AM*, and was included in Eyewear's *Best New British & Irish Poets 2016*. Her writing has received multiple nominations for the Pushcart Prize, with further nominations for the Queen's Ferry Press *Best Short Fictions*, Blazevox's *Bettering American Poetry, Best News Poets* [US] and the Derringer Awards, and was recently longlisted for the Royal Academy/Pindrop Short Story Award. In 2019, her debut poetry collection *DTR* (Broken Sleep) was nominated for the Forward Prize in two categories. She lives in London, where she is working hard on her novel.

INFLUX
PRESS

Influx Press is an independent publisher based in London, committed to publishing innovative and challenging literature from across the UK and beyond. Formed in 2012, we have published titles ranging from award-nominated fiction debuts and site-specific anthologies to squatting memoirs and radical poetry.

www.influxpress.com
@Influxpress

Lifetime supporters: Bob West and Barbara Richards